Chocolate Mousse For Greedy Goose

Written by
Julia Donaldson

Illustrated by
Nick Sharratt

MACMILLAN CHILDREN'S BOOKS

"Where's the meal?" asks hungry Seal.

"It's coming now," says busy Cow.

"What can I smell?" asks shy Gazelle.

"Macaroni," says Shetland Pony.

"Too hot for me!" says Chimpanzee.

"Blow on it, then," says Mother Hen.

"Carrots - yuck!" says fussy Duck.

"They're good for you," says Kangaroo.

"Chocolate mousse!" says greedy Goose.

"Don't just grab it," says angry Rabbit.

"I'll lick the bowl," says furry Mole.

"I'll lick it cleaner," laughs Hyena.

"It's all gone," says sad white Swan.

"I'll eat the cloth," says happy Moth.

"Let's wash up," says helpful Pup.

But lazy Sheep says, "No, let's . . .

. . . sle

For Amélie
J.D.

For Sasha and Joseph
N.S.

First published 2005 by Macmillan Children's Books
This edition published 2017 by Macmillan Children's Books
an imprint of Pan Macmillan
20 New Wharf Road, London N1 9RR
Associated companies throughout the world
www.panmacmillan.com

ISBN-13: 978-1-5098-7893-2

1 3 5 7 9 8 6 4 2

A CIP catalogue record for this book is available from the British Library.

Printed in China